May your jar be
filled with love
from all of your blessings!
Lisa S Hale
12007

Penny Love

Penny Love

written by Lisa Soares Hale

illustrated by Marilee Harrald-Pilz

ISBN 1-57921-844-X
Library of Congress Catalog Card Number: 2006900796
Printed in Korea

WINEPRESS WP PUBLISHING Kids

Dedication

For my precious girls, Corrina, Danielle, and Natalie
To my dearest mother, Dannia

One bright spring morning, Grandma was walking in the park with her granddaughter. Suddenly, they saw something shining in the sun.

"Look! A penny!" said Grandma. "Go and pick it up and know that Grandma loves you."

The little girl ran over and picked up the warm, brown penny. "I love you, too, Grandma," she said as she kissed her grandmother's cheek. "Can I keep it?"

"Oh, yes! And whenever you find a penny, you will know that Grandma loves you."

All the way home the little girl held the penny tight in her hand.

Grandma pulled an old jar out of the cupboard. "Every time you find a penny, put it in this jar. Soon you will *see* just how much Grandma loves you."

Through the years, the little girl found lots of warm, brown pennies.

She found one penny sparkling in the sand at the beach. She held it tight and whispered, "I love you, too, Grandma."

She found one penny waiting on the table at the ice cream parlor. She held it tight and whispered, "I love you, too, Grandma."

She found one penny hiding under the seat at the theater. She held it tight and whispered, "I love you, too, Grandma."

She even found one warm, brown penny lying among the rice thrown on her wedding day. The girl, now a lovely grown woman, picked up the penny and ran over to Grandma. She kissed her cheek and whispered, "I love you, too, Grandma."

Many, many years passed and the jar was overflowing with warm, brown pennies.

The girl grew older and now was a beautiful old woman with a granddaughter of her own.

And one spring morning she was walking in the park with her granddaughter, when suddenly they saw something shining in the sun. "What's that sparkle?" asked her granddaughter.

"Oh my! That's a warm, brown penny. Go and pick it up and know that I love you."

As her granddaughter ran to get the penny, the beautiful old woman smiled, looked toward heaven, and whispered, "I love you, too, Grandma!"

Tape your very own penny in the jar.

To order additional copies of

Penny Love

Have your credit card ready and call

Toll free: (877) 421-READ (7323)

or order online at: www.winepressbooks.com